On the Day the Tall Ships Sailed

On the Day the Tall Ships Sailed

by Betty Paraskevas and Michael Paraskevas

Simon & Schuster Books for Young Readers

As the tall ships made their way
Up the Hudson from the New York Bay,

Did you see him on the rim of the ridge?

Like a tiny dragonfly,
He was growing in the sky

Till he rested on Verrazano's bridge.

He was gallant, he was regal,
Did you see that eagle,
Eyes, canary diamonds in the sun?

Did you see his armor shine,
As the tall ships fell in line,
Moving up that river one by one?

Not a symbol done in stone
With a pillar for a throne;
Lifeless on a single dollar bill.

He was standing in the sky
As the tall ships moved on by.
He was flesh and blood that Sunday in July.

He was gallant, he was regal,
Did you see that eagle,
Eyes, canary diamonds in the sun?

Not a symbol done in stone.
He was flesh and blood and bone,
As he screamed above the thunder of the gun.

There were scars for times he failed,
But on the day the tall ships sailed,
Did you think of all the good things that he'd done?

Did you see him, were you proud
To be there in the crowd,

And was it good to be warm in the sun?

On the Day the Tall Ships Sailed

Slow Rock

As the tall ships made their way Up the
Hud-son from the New York __ Bay, Did you see him
on the rim of the ridge? Like a
tin-y dra-gon — fly, He was grow-ing in the __ sky Till he
rest-ed on __ Ver-ra-zan-o's __ bridge. He was
gal-lant, he was re-gal, Did you see that ea-gle,
Eyes, ___ ca-nar-y dia-monds in the __ sun? ___ Did you
see his ar-mor __ shine, As the tall ships fell in __ line,
Mov-ing up that __ riv-er __ one by one? ___ Not a
sym-bol done in __ stone With a pil-lar __ for a throne;

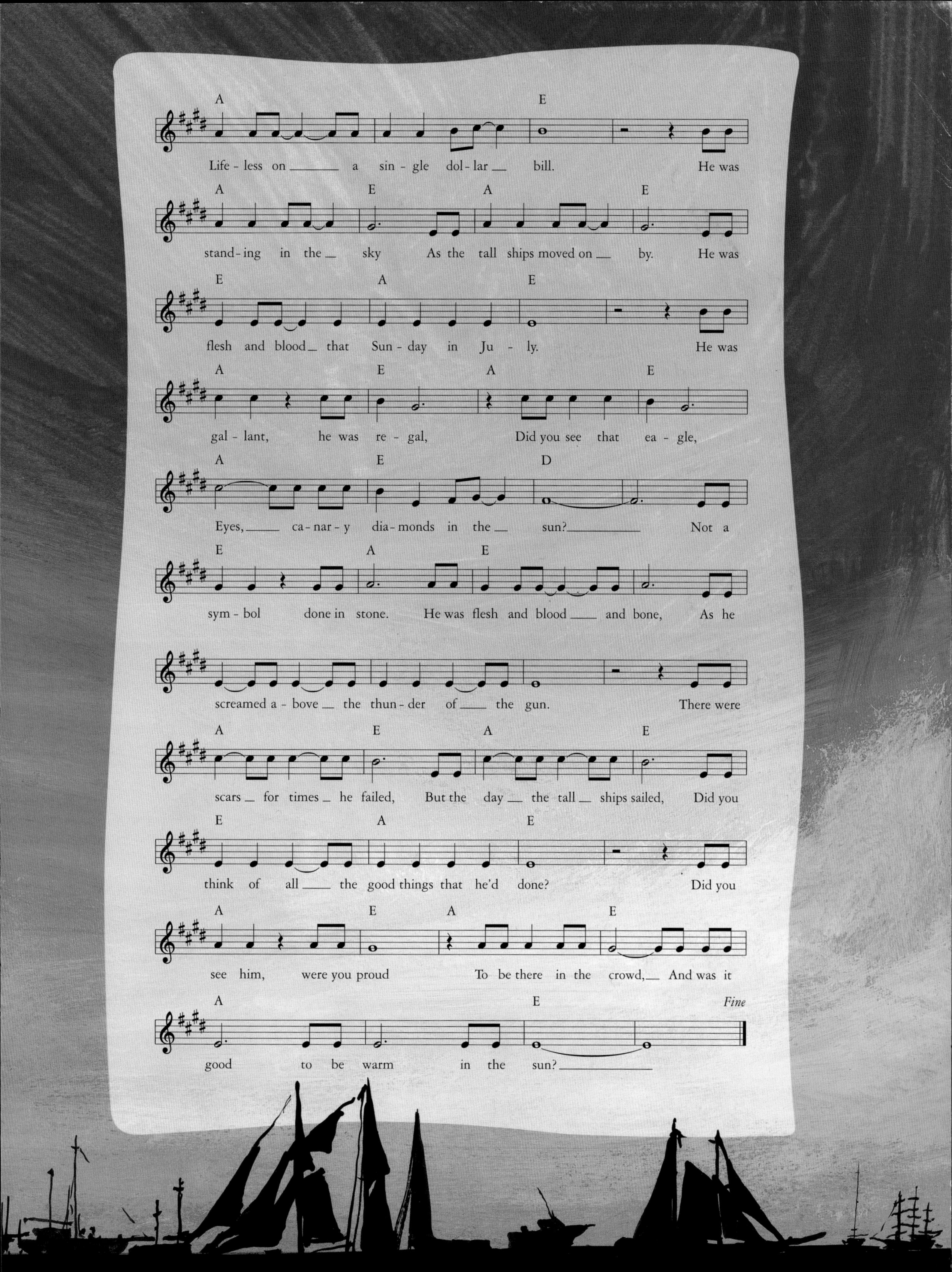
A E
Life - less on a sin - gle dol - lar bill. He was
A E A E
stand - ing in the sky As the tall ships moved on by. He was
E A E
flesh and blood that Sun - day in Ju - ly. He was
A E A E
gal - lant, he was re - gal, Did you see that ea - gle,
A E D
Eyes, ca - nar - y dia - monds in the sun? Not a
E A E
sym - bol done in stone. He was flesh and blood and bone, As he
screamed a - bove the thun - der of the gun. There were
A E A E
scars for times he failed, But the day the tall ships sailed, Did you
E A E
think of all the good things that he'd done? Did you
A E A E
see him, were you proud To be there in the crowd, And was it
A E
Fine
good to be warm in the sun?

To Danielle Maria Arturi, with sweetest memories

SIMON & SCHUSTER BOOKS FOR YOUNG READERS
An imprint of Simon & Schuster Children's Publishing Division
1230 Avenue of the Americas, New York, New York 10020

Book design by Jennifer Reyes
The text for this book is set in American Garamond.
The illustrations are rendered in acrylic on paper.
Printed in Hong Kong
2 4 6 8 10 9 7 5 3 1
Library of Congress Cataloging-in-Publication Data
Paraskevas, Betty.
On the Day the Tall Ships Sailed / Betty Paraskevas ;
illustrated by Michael Paraskevas.
p. cm.
Summary: As the tall ships sail into New York Harbor to celebrate the Fourth of July, a bald
eagle soars in the sky overhead, a regal symbol with shining armor and eyes like canary dia-
monds.
ISBN 0-689-82864-0
{1. Bald eagle—Fiction. 2. Eagles—Fiction. 3. New York (N.Y.)—Fiction. 4. Fourth of July—
Fiction. 5. Stories in rhyme.} I. Paraskevas, Michael, 1961-   ill. II. Title.
PZ8.3.P162Di 2000 [E]—dc21 99-22600 CIP